# A COUPLE OF BOYS
## HAVE THE
# BESTWEEKEVER

# MARLA FRAZEE

HARCOURT, INC.

ORLANDO · AUSTIN · NEW YORK · SAN DIEGO · LONDON · and MALIBU!

TO BILL, PAM, JAMES, and EAMON —
(OBVIOUSLY)

LIBRARY OF CONGRESS CATALOGING-IN-PUBLICATION DATA
FRAZEE, MARLA.
A COUPLE OF BOYS HAVE THE BEST WEEK EVER / MARLA FRAZEE
P. CM.
SUMMARY: FRIENDS JAMES AND EAMON ENJOY A WONDERFUL WEEK AT THE HOME OF EAMON'S
GRANDPARENTS DURING SUMMER VACATION.
(1. VACATIONS—FICTION. 2. FRIENDSHIP—FICTION. 3. GRANDPARENTS—FICTION. 4. BEACHES—FICTION.)
I. TITLE
PZ7.F866COU 2008
(E)—DC22 2006025781
ISBN 978-0-15-206020-6

FIRST EDITION

H G F E D C B A

PRINTED IN SINGAPORE

THE ILLUSTRATIONS IN THIS BOOK WERE DONE IN BLACK PRISMACOLOR AND GOUACHE
ON STONEHENGE PAPER.
THE DISPLAY AND TEXT LETTERING WERE DRAWN BY MARLA FRAZEE.
COLOR SEPARATIONS BY BRIGHT ARTS LTD., HONG KONG
PRINTED AND BOUND BY TIEN WAH PRESS, SINGAPORE

ONE HOT SUMMER DAY, JAMES WENT ON A
LONG DRIVE TO BILL AND PAM'S HOUSE SO HE COULD GO TO
A WEEK OF NATURE CAMP WITH HIS FRIEND EAMON.
BILL AND PAM ARE EAMON'S GRANDPARENTS.
THEY LIVE AT THE BEACH.

EAMON WAS ALREADY THERE.

NATURE CAMP WAS BILL'S IDEA.
BILL LOVED NATURE — ESPECIALLY COLD, WILD, AND
REMOTE PLACES WITH HARDLY ANY PEOPLE.
HE HAD BEEN TO MANY OF THESE SORTS OF PLACES BEFORE.
BUT THE PLACE HE MOST WANTED TO VISIT WAS ANTARCTICA
(BECAUSE OF THE PENGUINS).
PAM SAID SHE PREFERRED PEOPLE OVER PENGUINS.

EAMON THOUGHT THIS CHAT
WAS FASCINATING.
BUT HE HOPED JAMES
WOULD ARRIVE SOON.

DING DONG!

AND FINALLY, JAMES DID...

WITH JUST A COUPLE

OF HIS BELONGINGS.

HE HAD NEVER BEEN AWAY FROM HOME FOR AN ENTIRE WEEK, SO HE WAS VERY SAD WHEN HIS MOTHER DROVE AWAY.

BYE!

THE FIRST THING BILL WANTED TO DO BEFORE NATURE CAMP STARTED
WAS TO TAKE JAMES AND EAMON TO THE PENGUIN EXHIBIT AT THE
NATURAL HISTORY MUSEUM.
PAM OFFERED TO PACK A PICNIC OF PEANUT BUTTER-AND-HONEY SANDWICHES.
JAMES AND EAMON DISCUSSED THEIR OPTIONS.

THEY DECIDED TO STAY HOME AND ENJOY
BILL AND PAM'S COMPANY.

IN THE MORNING, BILL TOOK THE BOYS
TO NATURE CAMP.
THE ROAD WAS LONG AND CURVY.
JAMES AND EAMON LEARNED
A LOT OF NEW VOCABULARY WORDS
WHILE BILL DROVE.

ON THE WAY BACK THAT AFTERNOON, JAMES AND EAMON
DESCRIBED THEIR FIRST NATURE CAMP DAY TO BILL.

WHEN THEY GOT HOME, BILL UNROLLED A LARGE MAP OF ANTARCTICA
ON THE LIVING-ROOM FLOOR.

PAM GAVE JAMES AND EAMON COFFEE ICE-CREAM ICEBERGS WITH
HARD CHOCOLATE SAUCE ON TOP.

NATURE CAMP MADE THE BOYS VERY HUNGRY.

BILL BROUGHT TIDE CHARTS AND A GLOBE TO THE DINNER TABLE.
PAM SERVED BANANA WAFFLES WITH MAPLE SYRUP.

AT NIGHT, JAMES AND EAMON SLEPT
ON A BLOW-UP MATTRESS
WITH AN AUTOMATIC PUMP.

BILL AND PAM WONDERED IF THEY WOULD BE LONELY IN THE DOWNSTAIRS BEDROOM,

BUT THEY WEREN'T.

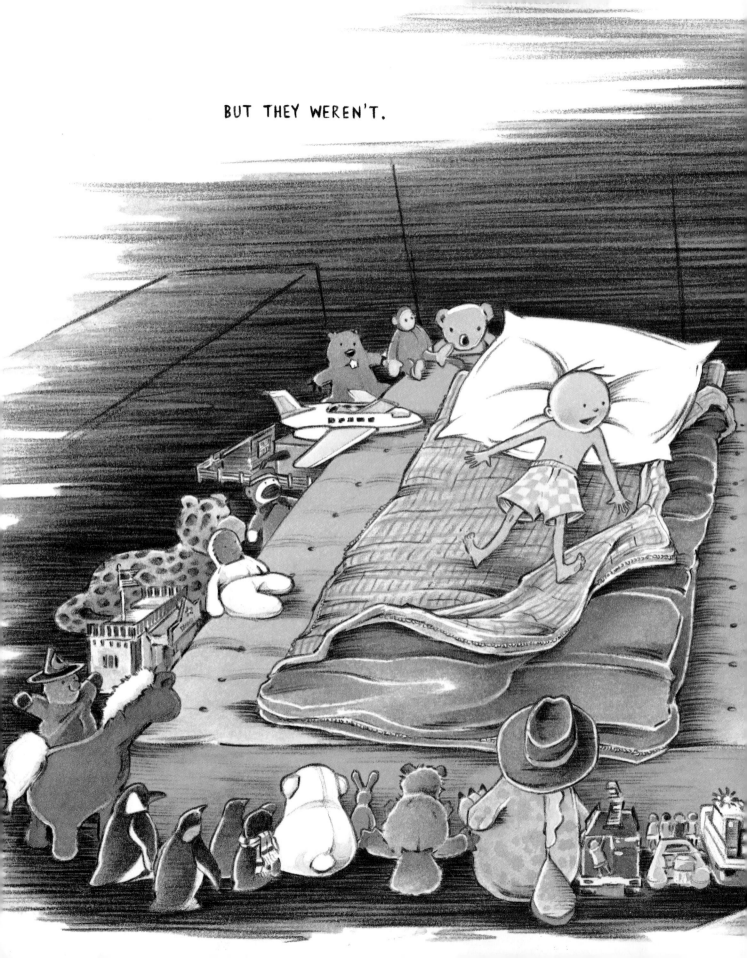

BEFORE THEY LEFT FOR NATURE CAMP THE NEXT MORNING,
BILL HANDED THEM EACH A PAIR OF BINOCULARS
AND A LIST OF BIRDS TO LOOK FOR.
ON THE WAY HOME, THE BOYS REPORTED THEIR FINDINGS.

AS THE NATURE CAMP WEEK
WENT BY, JAMES AND EAMON
PRACTICALLY BECAME ONE PERSON.
THEY DID EVERYTHING TOGETHER IN EXACTLY THE SAME WAY.
TO SAVE TIME, BILL BEGAN CALLING THEM JAMON.
HE WOULD SAY, "HEY JAMON, THINK ABOUT
WHETHER OR NOT YOU WANT TO SEE
THAT PENGUIN EXHIBIT."

AND JAMON WOULD THINK ABOUT IT.

THEN IN COMPLETE AGREEMENT, THE CAMPERS WOULD DECIDE
TO PRACTICE QUIET MEDITATION DOWNSTAIRS,

EAT MORE
BANANA WAFFLES,

AND ENJOY THE BEACH TOGETHER....

NATURE CAMP WAS JUST SO GREAT.

AND THEN ON FRIDAY AFTERNOON, NATURE CAMP WAS OVER.
JAMES AND EAMON RECAPPED THE WEEK DURING THE DRIVE HOME.

ON THEIR LAST NIGHT TOGETHER,
BILL, PAM, JAMES, AND EAMON HAD A POPCORN PARTY.
JAMES AND EAMON SOON DISCOVERED THAT A PARTY WITH
BILL AND PAM COULD GET PRETTY NOISY.

SO, THEY WANDERED OUTSIDE
FOR SOME PEACE AND QUIET.
TOMORROW THEY HAD TO GO HOME.

THEY LOOKED UP AT THE SKY AND OUT AT THE OCEAN.
FOR THE FIRST TIME ALL WEEK,
THEY COULDN'T THINK OF ANYTHING TO DO.
THE SUN WENT DOWN.
THE STARS CAME OUT.




THEN AT LAST, JAMES AND EAMON
FINALLY GOT REAL BUSY WITH SOMETHING...

AND IT TURNED OUT TO BE THE VERY BEST PART OF
THE BEST WEEK EVER.

BILL GAVE THE BOYS A BIG HUG.
HE SAID THIS WAS HOW PENGUINS HUDDLE TOGETHER
TO KEEP WARM.

PAM SAID SHE PREFERRED PEOPLE HUGS OVER PENGUIN HUDDLES.

JAMES AND EAMON HUGGED BILL AND PAM BACK (SORT OF).

AND WHEN THEIR MOMS FINALLY ARRIVED TO TAKE THEM HOME, JAMES AND EAMON GAVE EACH OTHER THE SECRET JAMON HANDSHAKE...

AND THEN THEY WALKED LIKE A COUPLE OF PENGUINS
ALL THE WAY OUT THE FRONT DOOR.

APR 2008

Caldecott Honor
Award 2009